W9-DES-534

Sailing to the Sea

by **Mary Claire Helldorfer**

Illustrated by **Loretta Krupinski**

Viking

VIKING
Published by the Penguin Group
Viking Penguin, a division of Penguin Books USA Inc.,
375 Hudson Street, New York, New York 10014, U.S.A.
Penguin Books Ltd, 27 Wrights Lane, London W8 5TZ, England
Penguin Books Australia Ltd, Ringwood, Victoria, Australia
Penguin Books Canada Ltd, 2801 John Street, Markham, Ontario, Canada L3R 1B4
Penguin Books (N.Z.) Ltd, 182–190 Wairau Road, Auckland 10, New Zealand

Penguin Books Ltd, Registered Offices: Harmondsworth, Middlesex, England

First published in 1991 by Viking Penguin, a division of Penguin Books USA Inc.

1 3 5 7 9 10 8 6 4 2

Library of Congress Cataloging in Publication Data
Helldorfer, Mary-Claire, 1954-
Sailing to the sea / by Mary Claire Helldorfer ;
illustrated by Loretta Krupinski.   p.   cm.
Summary: A young boy spends an exciting day
on his first sailboat journey with his aunt.
I S B N 0 · 6 7 0 · 8 3 5 2 0 · X : $ 1 2 . 9 5
[1. Sailboats—Fiction.   2. Sailing—Fiction.]
I. Krupinski, Loretta, ill.   II. Title.
PZ7.H37418Sai 1991 [E]—dc20   90-261CI

Printed in Singapore
Set in 14 point ITC Cushing Book
The artwork for this book was done in gouache
and colored pencil on three-ply bristol board.

"See you later, sailor," Mom calls,
and my little brother hugs me tight.
Everyone in the car waves: Grandad and my sisters,
squeezed between suitcases, beach chairs, and floats.
They're driving, but I'm sailing
from the river out to the sea.
"In three days, see you by the sea!"

The motor hums, my uncle's hand
rests on the boat's tiller.
"Hand up the dock lines," he says.
I do it! I do it!
Looking Glass clears the drawbridge.
My aunt raises the jib.

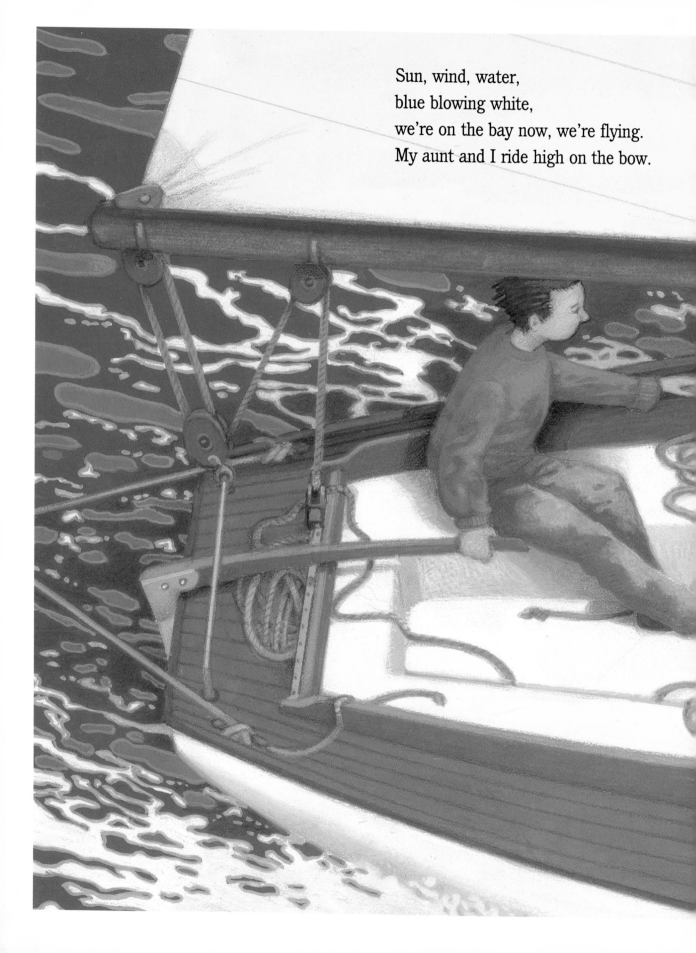

Sun, wind, water,
blue blowing white,
we're on the bay now, we're flying.
My aunt and I ride high on the bow.

Everything can be sat on, walked on—
cabin roof and cockpit seats.
I climb to the mast, shout orders down
to my uncle. I see his teeth,
but the wind snatches his laugh.

Straight ahead are double bridges:
steel spans cut the sky into puzzle pieces.
We sail in the shadows.
Whoosh, rumble, packed cars rush over our heads.
See you, see you, see you by the sea.

We anchor in a windless cove.
Looking Glass is still.
Our skins burn with a whole day's heat.
One by one we slip into the water
and swim in circles of gold.

Dark. I sleep in a pocket
below deck, in the curving bow
of the boat, resting on the waterline. . . .

Five A.M., creeping light.
A breeze, and honeysuckle
overflows its bank.

High noon, my aunt lifts her binoculars,
and sees an old dock, and a hill
dotted with pink.
We row and run and pick wild roses.

Two pirates, with pricked hands,
climb back onto *Looking Glass*.

Our compass needle swings north.
Everyone is sailing to the canal.
The freighters look like buildings
steaming by. Small tugs,
wearing tires on their lips,
pull barges low and long as the horizon.

The canal bridge stretches
like a roller-coaster track
high above the town and wharf.
We tie up, then climb steps
that zigzag up to the roadway.

Look down—our boat's a little bird
resting on the water.

At the canal restaurant I am given
the seat by the window.
Ships glide by in a slow parade.
I suck on crab legs.
It's funny to sit without rocking.

The freighters work all night,
and in their wake
we bump against the dock.
Their smokestacks nudge the moon.

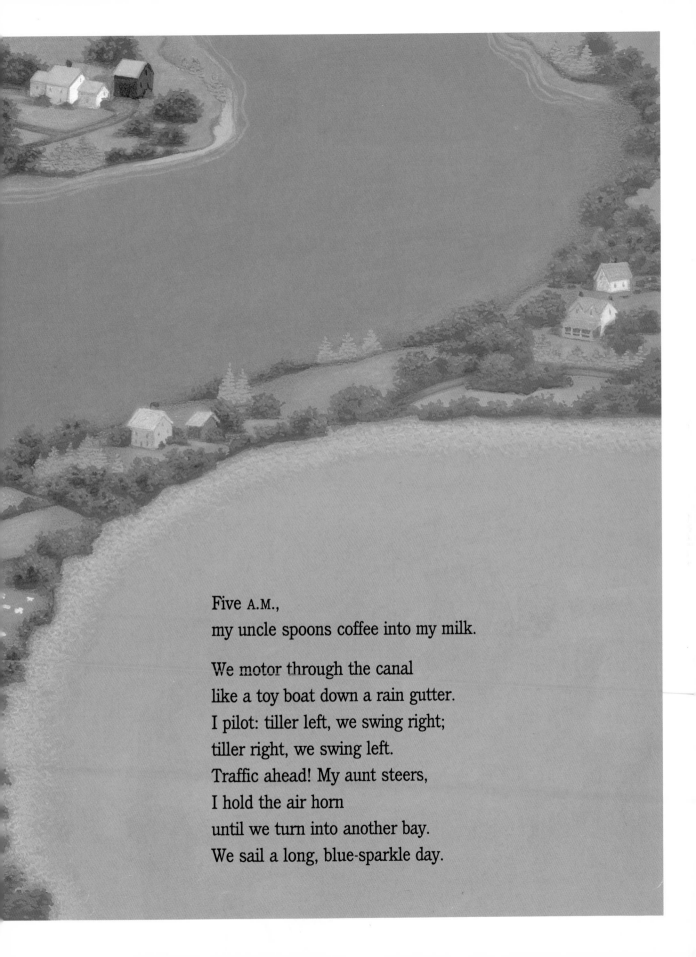

Five A.M.,
my uncle spoons coffee into my milk.

We motor through the canal
like a toy boat down a rain gutter.
I pilot: tiller left, we swing right;
tiller right, we swing left.
Traffic ahead! My aunt steers,
I hold the air horn
until we turn into another bay.
We sail a long, blue-sparkle day.

Late afternoon, my uncle points
to the west: squall line!
Radio on.
Charts out.
Sails down.
Hatches closed.
Life vests on.

In the galley I put away
soda cups and rolling fruit
just in time.

Lightning quivers. A wall of rain
moves across the water.
Looking Glass rides high,
smacks down on its belly.

My uncle is helmsman, my aunt, lookout.
Through the ports below
I watch the waves, tops blowing off.
The rigging whistles,
halyards clang against the mast.
Loud wind, and rain drums the deck above,
then only rain, splintery rain. . . .

"Can I come up?"

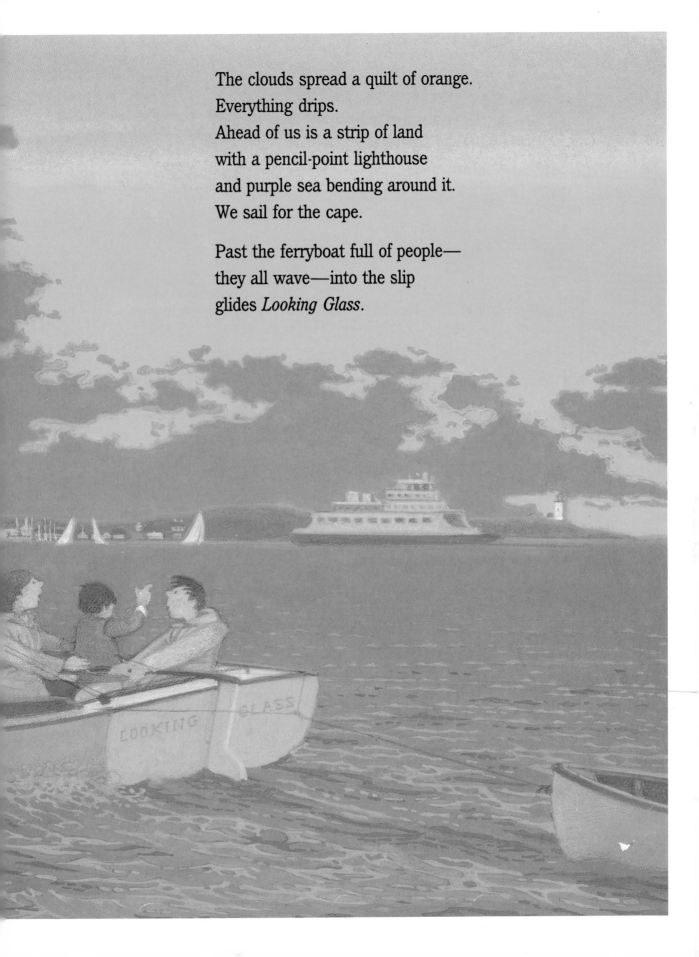

The clouds spread a quilt of orange.
Everything drips.
Ahead of us is a strip of land
with a pencil-point lighthouse
and purple sea bending around it.
We sail for the cape.

Past the ferryboat full of people—
they all wave—into the slip
glides *Looking Glass*.

We walk to the beach
where Mom and Grandad wait for us.
My sisters run and screech
like gulls: *See you, see you,
see you by the sea!*

My brother floats a little boat.
He sees me, hugs me hard.
I know he has been dreaming
of sailing to the sea.